The Martians Have Taken My Brother

Rowena Sommerville

RED FOX

Other titles by Rowena Sommerville:

Don't Step on that Earwig
If I Were a Crocodile

For My Friends' Children

A Red Fox Book

Published by Random House Children's Books
20 Vauxhall Bridge Road, London SW1V 2SA

A division of Random House UK Ltd
London Melbourne Sydney Auckland
Johannesburg and agencies throughout the world

Copyright © Rowena Sommerville 1993

3 5 7 9 10 8 6 4 2

First published in Great Britain by Hutchinson
Children's Books 1993

Red Fox edition 1994

Printed and bound in Great Britain by
Cox & Wyman Ltd, Reading, Berkshire

RANDOM HOUSE UK Limited Reg. No. 954009

ISBN 0 09 929331 5

Contents

My Mother's Purse

My mother's purse is stuffed with money,
it makes me feel all faint and funny,
if I took fifty pence or so,
I don't suppose she'd ever know;
it isn't like some major theft,
there's loads and loads of money left,
it isn't really, truly stealing –
so what's this awful sickly feeling?
I feel as though I've hurt my mum,
and all for chews and bubblegum.

Parting

Oh, won't you listen, darling child,
Hark to my words, my son,
How can you leave your doting Ma,
And you my cherished one?

Oh, do not hold me back, Mama,
For I must make my way,
Your love will travel at my side,
and widen day by day.

Oh, won't you listen, darling child,
My daughter and my boon,
How can you leave your doting Ma,
Who will be weeping soon?

Oh, do not cage me, Mother dear,
Or keep me so confined,
Your love will be a cloth to warm,
and not a thread to bind.

So all you young ones have to fly
to try new-feathered wings,
and, old ones, know that love can grow,
that stifles when it clings.

Grandad's Tree

We're planting a tree for my Grandad,
we've done it to help us recall
the hours he spent in his garden,
and the way that he thought of us all.

We didn't see Grandad too often,
he lived such a long way away,
and now that he's gone there are so many things
that I wish I had bothered to say;

But Mum says he knew that we loved him,
and how very much he loved us,
and he wouldn't have liked big, emotional scenes,
and he wouldn't have wanted a fuss;

So we're planting a tree for my Grandad,
it's our way of saying Goodbye,
and its roots will reach down to the life-giving earth,
and its branches will stretch to the sky.

Some People's Brothers

Some people's brothers are better than others,
and most people's brothers are better than mine;
the size of those boys and the noise of their toys,
well, it's sending me into an early decline.
How I hate what they do and the way that they chew,
and the things that they say and the smell of their feet,
and unless they're all gone before Neighbours is on,
you can wheedle and whine, but you won't get a seat.

Oh, the way that they act and their absence of tact,
and the trivial talk about football all night,
and their primeval grunts and their juvenile stunts,
and the way that they're constantly threatening to fight.

All my friends say it's great, you can meet all their mates,
but I don't think there's one of them's got what it takes,
and I don't want to marry some Tom, Dick or Harry
I'll live on my own and breed poisonous snakes,

'cos I don't think I oughta impose on a daughter
the things that this family imposes on me,
and I know I sound hateful and coldly ungrateful,
but fate pulled a pretty mean trick, you'll agree;
because some people's brothers are better than others,
and some people's brothers may even be worse,
but I want it stated, that being related,
through mothers to brothers,
is really a *curse!*

Between

I'm growing up, I'm big and tough,
my back is strong, my voice is rough,
I've said goodbye to soppy stuff;
I don't need comfort any more,
I'm not the child I was before,
I'm standing at my own life's door;
the world is begging me to go,
I want to see, I want to know,
I welcome life and learning, so
just let the future blaze.

But sometimes in the dark of night,
the moment I turn off the light,
I feel a sweaty, sickly fright;
my heart beats faster than it should,
I don't call out, although I could,
I hug myself, but that's no good;
and in a corner of my mind,
among abandoned toys, I find
a boy who wants to stay behind
in softer, simpler days.

Porridge in the Keyboard
For Eddie and Cade

Oh, please don't hit me, brother dear,
Don't punch me on the hooter,
But I confess,
I've made a mess,
All over your computer!

So clean it up, you mucky pup,
Or this will be the end-o,
You must restore
My Commodore,
Or I'll take your Nintendo!

Luck

Harrikins Larrikins, oh what a boy!
Clearly he's Mummikins' own pride and joy;
Willikins Spillikins, nearly as good,
but somehow the world doesn't care as it should;
Sallikins Ballikins, oh what a pearl!
Goodness and loveliness shine from each curl;
Pattikins Mattikins, nearly as sweet,
but somehow the world doesn't fall at her feet;
So many babykins, so many tots,
each of them hoping that they'll be loved lots;
So many little ones swarming the earth,
each with their portion of fortune at birth;
Some achieve glory and some achieve fame,
but there's no referee overseeing *this* game,
and life can be cruel, it can't be denied
so you better just hope you've got luck on your side!

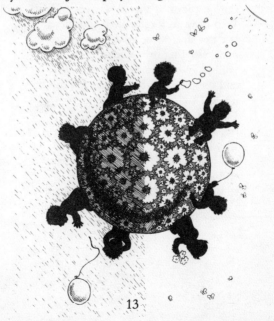

Fuzzbuzz!

Say, look at that, Ma, I've got hair!
Where once I was childishly bare,
it's suddenly started to grow,
I wonder how soon it will show –
does it make me look manly and brave?
Should I set the clock early to shave?
Any day I'll be driving in cars,
I'll be ordering drinks in bars,
I'll be raving in clubs,
misbehaving in pubs,
I'll be chillin'-out under the stars;
but just call me a child if you dare,
'cos look at that, Ma, I've got hair!

Oh, just look at that, Ma, I've got hair!
Well okay, so it's just here and there,
but this shadowing under my arms
demonstrating my pubescent charms,
will be giving out hormones galore,
and the girls will be swooning I'm sure –
They'll say *isn't he sweet?*
I'll be mobbed in the street,
not a one will resist me,
they'll queue up to kiss me,
the whole world will fall at my feet;
and it isn't a dirt-mark, I swear,
so just look at me, Ma, I've got hair!

Grandad's Hair

How much do I love Grandad?
A hug for every hair –
And don't think I don't care much,
'cos you don't see many there –
his head may shine as smooth as eggs,
but you should see his hairy legs!

Blessings

Shelley Parker's bedroom carpet
is soft and pink and fluffy,
and all her bedroom furniture
matches.
Shelley Parker's hair is long,
her Mum lets her frizz it,
and even then she can sit on it.
Shelley Parker's brother
is good-looking,
and he plays in the football team,
and he lets her go about with him.

Our headmaster says
we should count our blessings,
and think of homeless people,
and all the starving children in Africa,
and I do, I do,
but then I think of
Shelley Parker's bedroom carpet,
and I count some of her blessings too.

Slow Jeanie

There is this girl in my class called Jeanie.
She doesn't play with anybody much.
She is still on early readers.
Sometimes she does good pictures,
but she is not careful.
Sometimes she wears the same jumper for days,
even though it is dirty.
Sometimes she cries in dinners,
even though she is not a little one.
Nobody came to see her in the play,
even though she was Mrs. Noah,
and she saw the rainbow first.
At the end of school we run out of the gate like marbles,
but slow Jeanie creeps home in inches.

Jamie

Jamie in the mornings,
waiting for the bus,
no jacket and no breakfast
and nobody makes a fuss.

Jamie in the evenings,
making toast for tea,
doesn't matter what he eats,
there's no-one there to see.

Jamie in the summer,
roaming far and wide,
an independent traveller,
just his shadow at his side.

Jamie in the winter,
shrinking in his skin,
no-one's looking out for him
and no-one's waiting in.

Jamie's wise and watchful,
he's sharp and hard as stone,
he knows you mustn't stumble,
when you walk the world alone.

My Best Friend

I've got a friend
and we play 'let's pretend',
and he chases me round with a stick,
and he acts really mad,
and pretends to be bad,
and I have to run away quick;
and he's ever so tough,
and he plays really rough,
and he doesn't like reading or toys,
and if you're in his gang
you can talk special slang,
and you're better than ordinary boys;
and my friend's really strong,
when he does something wrong,
he never says sorry or cries,
and I'm a bit weak,
and I'm too shy to speak,
and I sometimes get tears in my eyes;
my friend is called Roy,
he's a really big boy,
and he says that he'll make my arm bend,
and I'm running away,
that's enough for today,
and I wish Roy was not my best friend!

Party Smarty

My parents gave a party,
and loads of people came,
but how they'll face the world again
without eternal shame,
I'll never know.
The huge amount of food they ate,
the vast amount they drank –
old Gert the goldfish looks relieved
she's left with half a tank
(and that's got crumbs in).
The things that they were wearing,
the things I overheard –
(I didn't understand it all,
but I got it word for word,
I'll tell you later.)
The people from the takeaway
brought loads of home-made wine,
and Jason Baker's mother's friend,
kept shouting, 'I feel fine!'
('til he fell over).
The man who runs the betting shop
was capering in his kilt,
until he tried the highland fling
just where the wine was spilt.
(He's got no secrets.)
The people from three houses down,
who said they wouldn't stop,
danced on the lawn 'til nearly dawn,
until they had to drop
(I won't say what).

Mrs. Taylor did a tango
with a rosebud and a shawl,
she was amateur but eager,
and I think she gave her all
(or so I heard, anyway).
Then Councillor Mrs. Kershaw
came round about the row,
and in the end she wouldn't go.
(I bet she's still here now,
just snoring gently.)
The people from the old folks' home
were playing postman's knock,
with one or two adjustments
which gave us quite a shock.
(So energetic!)
And Shirley Vernon's parents came,
they're normally so quiet,
then someone shouted LIMBO!
and they were the first to try it –
(luckily my mum's a nurse).
Doctor Bright and Mrs. Lewis
sparked off quite a big sensation,
though they said that they were practising
first aid resuscitation –
(just in case, they said).
Mr. Collins led the conga,
dancing out into the night,
it's a shame he got arrested,
though he put up quite a fight
(well, for a vicar);
and still the joint was jumping,
they were bouncing off the wall,
they were capering and cavorting,
'til a voice said, 'Evening, all'
(he lost his helmet);

but then the final drink was drunk,
the final record played,
the final bleary guest went home
(except for those who stayed
where they had fallen).
I spent all Sunday clearing up,
and Dad said, 'Well done, son,'
I said I thought it most unfair –
I mean, who'd had the fun? –
Dad said, 'It wasn't all that good,
you didn't miss much, kiddio,'
I said, 'I didn't miss a thing,
and I got it all on video!'
And *that* surprised him, I could tell.

The New Boyfriend

My mother's got a new boyfriend,
I suppose that I think he's all right,
you can certainly see that *she's* happy,
it's like someone turned on the light.
I don't really know why she wants him,
I mean, after all, she's got us,
but now she's all giggly and girly,
you just wouldn't credit the fuss.
She says that she thinks she's entitled
to her own bit of friendship and fun,
but I must say that I
am confused as to why
she's decided that he is the one.
She could have done worse, I admit it,
and sometimes he can be quite sweet,
and you wouldn't actually laugh or feel sick
if you saw him walk past in the street.
But, once, I caught them both kissing,
and it did make me feel very strange,
'cos I thought that we were all right as we were,
but Mum says it's time for a change.
I guess that I'll come to accept him,
it's mostly a question of time,
and I know that my mum
wants to be with someone
before she gets well past her prime.
So now, slowly, we're getting acquainted –
well, we're having to, like it or no,
and if he does stay,
I suppose it's okay,
but if I had MY way –
he could go!

Tessa's Dream

Tessa's sound asleep,
she lies
curled up tight,
she softly sighs;
then the dragon comes,
she cries,
air around her burns.
Tessa turns to face,
defies,
looks into the smoke-dark eyes,
recognises
hope.
She offers a small hand to stroke,
she tries for friendship,
and the stars in space
become a rope of sparks.
Her dragon yields at this,
it kneels;
fearlessly combined
they rise and rise,
higher, on,
they fly and fly,
through the roaring, fiery skies.

Tessa greets the day,
it brings
sudden memories of wings,
lingering surprise.

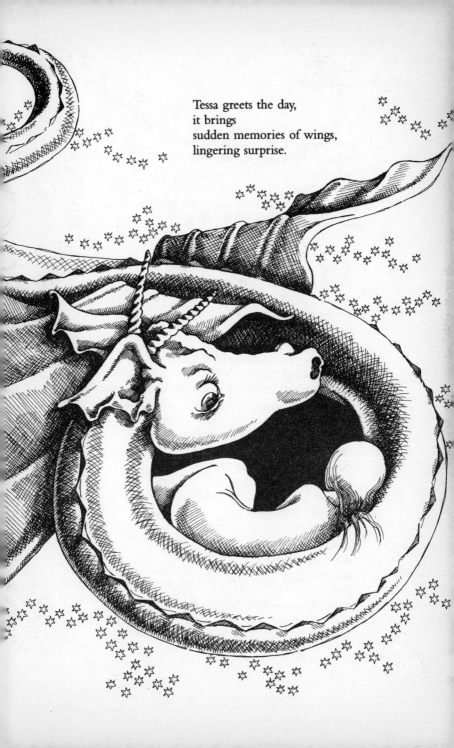

Sisterlist

My big sister says she loves me,
says she'll take me round the town,
Mum says, 'Ooh, you are a brick,
you never let your old ma down.
Now I won't be long, I promise,
get yourselves some chips to eat',
gives my sister something extra,
'that's 'cos you deserve a treat,
and I know that I can trust you,
be good girls and please don't fight';
as she closed the door, my sister
pointed at me and said,
                              'RIGHT –
don't imagine that I like you,
I'm just giving Mum a hand,
I can't go if I don't take you,
and I need the money and
don't you walk too close behind me,
don't wear knee-socks or a hat,
please don't pose or pick your nose,
and don't you look at me like that,
don't ask me to go in toyshops,
you can see I'm much too hip,
don't wear clothes that look as though
they came from Oxfam's lucky dip,
if we see some tasty lads
then please attempt some sort of cool,
and don't embarrass me by smirking
if we meet some kids from school,
and don't go touching things in Woolworths,
don't you wear that gruesome coat,
and when I'm chatting with my friends
don't cough, or hum, or clear your throat,
and don't start whingeing that you're bored,

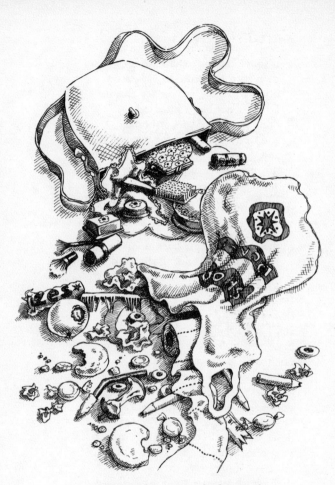

or moaning that you've had enough,
and don't tell me you've got a blister,
learn to bear it, life is tough,
don't go pulling funny faces,
don't go asking me for dosh,
and if you're spoken to, act normal,
don't talk common, don't talk posh,

and don't butt in on conversations,
don't ear-hole the things we say,
if some nice boy chats me up,
then have the sense to walk away,
don't go asking me for ice cream,
DON'T act like a little kid,
don't go telling tales at home,
and don't blame me for what YOU did,
and don't tell Mum I'm wearing lipstick,
no-one likes a dirty sneak,
and if you give me any grief
I'll beat you up at school next week.'

Well, all of this went on for ages,
then we heard the back door key,
Mum came in, said, 'Back so soon, girls?
Who'll make me a cup of tea?
Are you two behaving well?
Was that a quarrel that I heard?'
and then I looked at my big sister,
but I didn't say a word.

Not Fair

Well, I don't think it's fair at all,
it's not fair, no, it's not;
you give me such a little,
and you give her such a lot.

And I don't think it's right at all,
it's not right, it's a shame,
and even when she starts it,
then it's me that gets the blame.

And I don't have to live here,
you can sit and watch me go,
I hate my little sister
and I always will do, so

I'm living in the garden,
and I'm never coming back,
I don't want you for my mother
and I'm giving you the sack –

'Cos you never treat us equal,
and you always treat me worst,
and I wish you would remember
that I was your baby first.

What You Get From a Dog

When everyone's picking on someone,
when tension lies heavy as smog,
when I'm feeling ignored,
or I'm lonely or bored,
that's when I turn to the dog.

When the world seems too busy to bother,
when no human wants me for a chum,
there's a pal I can call,
with no trouble at all –
and to think we call animals dumb!

There's a shake-a-paw, catch-a-ball comfort,
a nose-on-the-knee kind of mate,
you can act like a nut
with your mongrel or mutt,
and they'll still think you're groovy and great.

Now, I'm not a believer in heaven,
and yet dogs deserve one, I'd say,
some celestial ground
they can rampage around,
and play waggy-tail-smelly all day.

So, I'm not making fun of your fishes,
your mynah, your mouse or your mog,
but love undeserved,
unrefined, unreserved,
that's what you get from a dog!

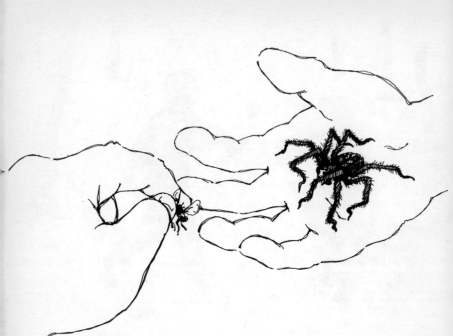

A Brief Passion

My brother caught a spider,
and he kept it as a pet,
and he took it all the creepy-crawly creatures he could get,
and he kept it in his bedroom by the bookcase in a box,
where it lived among the lego
and the dustballs and the socks.
My mother said she hated it,
she said it had to go,
but my brother, he said absolutely, definitely *NO!*
He said he loved the spider and the way it zapped about,
and that he'd leave home as well
if someone threw the spider out.

My mother, she was tempted for a moment, then she thought
and considered all the critters
that my brother's spider caught,
and though she didn't like it,
she agreed that it could stop
(but if it gave her trouble,
then she'd squash it with the mop).
My brother used to chat to it
and feed it bits of fly,
he'd sit there quite contented watching tiny creatures die,
and the spider led a life of unimaginable ease,
with my brother always petting it
and grovelling on his knees.
Soon the spider hardly moved,
apart from wrapping things in thread,
'cos my brother did the hunting,
and the catching part instead,
and it didn't run about, just sort of sat there getting fat,
and my brother lost all interest and he said,
'I'm bored with that',
then he tidied up his bedroom, 'cos he needed space to play,
and he went and got the hoover
and he cleared the lot away!

Mashie

Mashie was my huggylove,
Mashie was my friend,
Mashie used to drive my poor old mother
round the bend,
'cos everywhere I had to go
my Mashie had to come,
and everything I had to eat
my Mashie wanted some;
he was better than a blanket,
or a bunny or a bear,
'cos, though no-one else could see him,
still, *I* knew that he was there;
and every journey in the car
my Mashie had a place,
and everybody else was squashed
to give my Mashie space;
and every journey into town,
I had to make a fuss,
'cos people sat on Mashie
when we travelled on the bus.
I used to share with Mashie
when I played out on the swings,
I used to tell old Mashie
all my special secret things;
I used to talk to Mashie
when I lay awake in bed,
my mother got to thinking
I was funny in the head!

And then Susannah came to tea,
she had a heart of steel,
she said that Mashie was not nice,
and was not even *real*.
And from that moment poor old Mash
began to fade away
and was not quite so pleasing
when I called him up to play,
and soon it seemed that only I
remembered Mashie's name,
but even on our own, you know,
it didn't feel the same.

So now I know that friends can change,
and sometimes drift apart,
but there'll always be a little place for Mashie
in my heart.

First Loves

I'm in love, I am, with Martin,
though I've been too shy to speak,
but I love his curly lashes,
and the freckles on his cheek,
although sometimes I love Phillip,
'cos he stands so tall and strong,
and he tells those awful stories
that just carry you along,
and on the bus I saw a boy
who turned me to a wreck,
though I sat behind him just the once,
and I only saw his neck,
and I did love Mr. Collins,
'cos he's always really kind,
but he's old and bald and married,
so I've put him from my mind,
and I really liked that footballer
who scored and won the cup,
but I couldn't stand the football,
so I had to give him up,
and you know that gorgeous singer,
well, I couldn't eat my tea,
'cos he looked into the camera,
and I know he winked at me,
and I love that man on telly
who does all the fiddly bits,
in between the proper programmes,
but my mother says that it's
not the real, true thing at all,
it's puppy love, and so
I'll fancy someone else tomorrow,
but I say
What do mothers know?

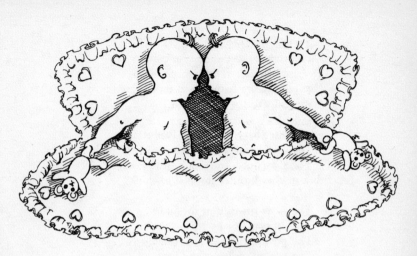

Paul and Peter Rappaport

Paul and Peter Rappaport
Were twins, but not the happy sort;
In school, in play, in love, in sport,
In every field of life, they fought.

Their parents rapidly grew tired
Of all the discipline required
To quell the monsters they had sired,
And, when the twins turned ten, expired.

The boys then ran completely mad,
And every guardian they had
Departed, saying, 'Though it's sad,
I cannot stay, they are too bad.'

The twins fought through their growing years,
With prods and punches, jibes and jeers,
With blackened eyes and battered ears,
It was fore-doomed to end in tears.

Each brother did the best he could
To harm the other, though no good
Can come from hatred, and they should
Have realised that evil would:

– The aftershave that made Paul stink
– The joke-shop soap that turned Pete pink
– The sharpened knives left in the sink
(but neither brother stopped to think)

– The rusty tin-tack in the shoe
– The slippers lined with superglue
– The powdered gravel in the stew
– The poison spider in the loo

– The threatening letters sent to friends
– The loosened chimney that descends
– The brakes that fail on hairpin bends
we know where such behaviour ends.

And so the vicious pattern set,
But worse, of course, would follow yet,
For Pete had got a much-loved pet
(A passion he would soon regret)

For Paul stole Peter's dog away,
And left it on the motorway –
A crime for which they both would pay,
And look out, here comes judgement day!

The brothers faced each other then,
Identically angry men,
Each hating with the strength of ten,
But battle hardly started when –

Their younger sister Eleanor
(Forgot to mention her before),
Saw just the chance she'd waited for
And handed both a double bore.

(Now, just in case you've missed the plot,
I should explain the family'd got
A small estate, a lovely spot,
A sole survivor'd bag the lot!)

Bad blood rushed to each brother's head,
They loaded unfraternal lead,
Then turned and shot each other dead –
And on their grave in stone it said

That: 'Paul and Peter Rappaport
Were twins but not the happy sort;
In every field of life they fought,
But life proved shorter than they thought.'

The moral of this tale is plain:
Avoid the dreadful fate of Cain,
Don't sock your sibling, use your brain –
When brothers fight, then others gain!

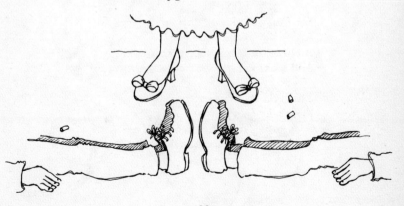

Disappointment

Tearing paper,
ripping thread,
Christmas presents
on my bed;
scrabbling tissue,
pulling string,
get the goodies,
that's the thing!
Toys and treasures
all around,
on the pillow,
on the ground;
gifts and glories
piling high,
what a lucky child am I!
So much money
gladly spent,
so much love and kisses sent;
so much kindness,
so much thought,
so I know I really ought
to be overwhelmed with glee,
but, inside, it's still
just
me.

Now, I know that I sound selfish,
like a spoilt, ungrateful brat,
all I'm saying is – the promise
makes reality seem flat.
All that shiny Christmas paper,
all that tinsel, all that fizz,
all those adverts on the telly,
telling you how great life is;
when you open up your parcels
and discover what's inside,
does it change the world forever?
Could it be the adverts lied?
Even though I longed for Christmas,
craved it all for weeks before,
now it's come and still I'm wanting
something else, or something more.
Told my mother,
she said, 'Listen –
life won't change because of *things*,
prize your gifts,
and prize the wisdom
disappointment sometimes brings.'

Beads

Rewiring our new house,
I found a tin of beads
lodged in old circuitry
beneath a dusty floorboard,
hidden by an earlier child
who climbed these stairs
and woke to these windows,
before we knew the house existed.

The house memory activated mine,
as beads spilled over the floor
to windy tarmac,
where chains of girls
skipped and danced
in a long-forgotten playground.
We had a craze for swapping beads –
I plundered bracelets and brooches,
carrying my treasures to school
in preciously padded tins.

Now those dancers are scattered and spread,
and I have children,
creating their own particular archaeology
in this house.

Our histories are ropes
of dull and diamond days;
just occasionally,
we rediscover pieces of the pattern
in accidental networks.
Linking beads
can make a necklace,
linking words
can make a poem,
linking people
can make a family,
it's simply a matter of connecting correctly,
as every electrician knows.

Leave Me Alone

So how was your school today, Robert, my own,
So how was your school today, Robert McPhee?
Oh, school was all right, Mother,
Leave me alone,
I don't want to think of it,
Now that I'm free.

And how was your lunch today, Robert, my own,
And how was your lunch today, Robert McPhee?
My lunch was all right, Mother,
Leave me alone,
My lunch was as all right
As school lunch can be.

And how were your friends today, Robert, my own,
And how were your friends today, Robert McPhee?
My friends were all right, Mother,
Leave me alone,
Why do you have to keep
Bothering me?

And what did you learn today, Robert, my own,
And what did you learn today, Robert McPhee?
I learnt quite a lot of things,
Leave me alone,
I'm resting my brain now,
I'm watching TV.

It's time for your bed I think, Robert, my own,
It's time for your bed I think, Robert McPhee,
Oh, don't make me go up to bed
All alone,
How cold and unfeeling you mothers can be,
I want to stay here and sit talking, you see,
I'm starting to think
You don't care about me!

Manners
A mother speaks

Now, we're just here for a short time,
best behaviour if you can,
all these elderly relations
want to meet a nice young man.

Uncle Norman's got a problem,
please don't stare, don't be so rude,
just because he makes those noises,
doesn't mean he hates his food.

Aunty Florence didn't mean it,
yes, I saw her pinch your cheek,
don't keep making such a fuss,
it couldn't hurt, her hands are weak.

Shush, now, yes, I saw Aunt Molly
stroking Mr. Thompson's knee,
no, don't tell your Uncle Peter,
just forget it, leave it be.

Aunty Dora isn't drunk, dear,
yes, I know her face is red,
yes, I heard her in the kitchen,
no, it's not true what she said.

Yes, I see that Grandpa's snoozing,
yes, his beard is full of crumbs,
yes, his teeth are very shiny,
no, they don't quite fit his gums.

Well, I think we must be going,
and of course we'll come again,
yes, it's been a lovely visit,
manners, please, say thank you, Ben.

In My Castle

My mother's very beautiful,
my father's like a king,
I live inside a castle,
and there's loads of everything.

I wear a dress that sparkles,
I wear a golden crown,
and everybody cheers to see me
riding round the town.

Though I'm sitting in my bedroom,
I can go there in my mind,
I just say the magic password,
and the real world's left behind,

And there's flowers and there's fountains
and there's always sunny skies,
and no-one's ever angry,
and no-one ever cries.

So why is Daddy shouting?
And why is Mummy sad?
Have I done something naughty?
Have I done something bad?

I can hear them in the kitchen,
I can hear them through the wall,
but when I'm in my castle
I can't hear them at all,
so I'm staying in my castle
and I won't hear them at all.

The Shame of It

Oh, lummy, Mum,
you look a mess,
please don't wear trainers with that dress!
Oh, blimey, Dad,
it's Mister Sad,
was that the only shirt you had?
I live with THEM,
we share a name,
will people think that I'm to blame?
And oh, the fear,
the squirming fright,
please let me die on parents' night.
Around the town
I walk behind
in dread that kids who know me find
the awful truth:

That THEY're with me,
yet everywhere I seem to see
that other kids
have normal folks,
who dress OK and tell good jokes,
and drive nice cars,
and act real cool,
and don't embarrass them in school;
or could it be
they feel the same –
is this some universal shame?
and when I'm grown,
and I'm a dad,
will my kids think that I'm that bad?

Conjunctions

Rosie is my best friend,
we were very close until
she went and told Rhiannon
I was going out with Bill;
now I was keen on Jamie
and I tried to hold his hand,
but he said I was soppy
and he fancied Sarah and
he asked her to his party,
but she didn't want to go,
'cos she thought he was bigheaded
and she ran away, and so
he spread it round the playground
she'd been holding hands with Ben,
and that got her in trouble
'cos Aqeela heard it when
she went into the cloakroom
to get something from her coat,

and because she's after Ben,
she got poor Sarah by the throat;
so we ran to get a teacher
who came very quickly but
they were fighting in the toilets
and the toilet door was shut,
so the teacher got quite angry
and she pointed out that if
they didn't cut the volume
the whole school would hear the tiff,
then she told me off for laughing
and she sent me out to play,
but I felt weary after
such a complicated day;
so I hung about and sat about
and walked about and then
I said Hello to Rosie
and we made it up again.

The Martians Have Taken My Brother

The Martians have taken my brother,
I must say I'm glad that they did,
I know it seems hard on my mother,
but he was such a pain of a kid.

He kept pinching things from the larder,
he kept making smells in the loo,
and though I tried harder and harder,
I just couldn't like him – could you?

The Martians have got him well hidden
(he's locked in the shed for the day),
And Dad says the shed is forbidden,
so I've thrown the shed key away.

I know that he'll bang on the window,
I know that he'll yell and he'll shout,
I think that he'll have to stay in though,
'cos the Martians just won't let him out!

Oh dear! Mum's back from the shop now,
I've seen her walk in through the gate,
I suppose all the fun has to stop now,
Oh no! – she's come in – it's too late!

I wish I could rescue my brother,
I wish I could unlock the shed,
'cos if I get caught by my mother
She might put me in there instead!

Big Kids

I've got this sort of cousin,
her name is Nicola,
my mum says that when she was born
something went wrong,
so though she's quite big
she's like a little kid really.
Some people call her Loonytunes,
and I think that she thinks
they're being friendly.
She doesn't get mad,
she just smiles.
In some ways the joke's on them,
I mean they're calling out bad names,
and she's happy, right?
One time I got into a fight over her,
these boys said,
'She's your cousin, you must be loonytunes too',
and I didn't know what to do, or say.
I had to run away,
there was a whole gang of them.
Then I wished that she wasn't my cousin
or she wasn't loonytunes,
but that's life my mum says,
you can't understand it,
it isn't what you planned.
Nicola comes round most Sundays,
and the other week it was my birthday;
we were playing musical chairs,
and my mum said,
'Let Nicky play',
and she went all red
so I had to let her
and all my friends were looking,
you know, in that way;

And then she won, fair and square,
she did,
no kidding,
and her face was like she'd won the pools,
and I thought we were cruel before.
Then we brought in the cake
and everybody sang Happy Birthday,
and my dad said,
'Let Nicky blow the candles out as well',
so we lit them again
and she had a go.
She was so pleased,
it was like giving her a present,
and I thought, it doesn't take much to make her happy,
and that's a sort of gift.
I've got a photo of that party,
there's Mum and Dad and Nicola
and all my friends and me,
and we're all being silly,
like a bunch of big kids really.

Twinnies
For Sandra and Sue

Aren't they sweet, the little twinnies,
In their matching frilly pinnies;
Isn't it so very nicey,
Such a lovely girly twicey!

What a pair of bouncing boyses,
Twice the jokes and twice the joyses,
Face the future at the double,
Twice the work and twice the trouble!

If you see them, you say crikey!
Each to both is so alikey!
Could not tell the one from t'other,
Like the pod-pea and its brother!

All our lives the people staring,
First exclaiming, then comparing –
One of you is sporty/runny,
One of you is naughty/funny,
One of you must be the older,
One of you must be the bolder,
One of you must be the wise one,
One of you must be the prize one.

All our lives we've had to bear it,
Just as well there's two to share it,
Such a lot of cheesey grins
Greet you, when you're one of twins.

Christmas, Mardy 1946
For Robbie

Thomas Robbins was my Grandpa,
Loved the world, despite its sin,
When he saw the homeless stranger,
Praised the Lord, and took him in.

In Mardy in the freezing winter,
German prisoners in the camp,
Captured in the war, and kept there,
Chilled by dirt, defeat and damp.

We would see them, walking daily
On permitted exercise,
I had thought them less than human –
War necessitates these lies.

We sat round the Christmas table,
Laden with the kitchen's wealth,
Thanked the Lord and thanked each other,
Said Good luck, Good cheer, Good health.

Grandpa raised a hand for silence,
Said, 'God's Grace must be made real,
While those men are loveless, lonely,
We should choke to eat this meal.'

Marched down to the wire encampment,
Gave his message, stood to wait,
While we children stared, made quiet
By the spiked, forbidding gate.

When the guard returned he said
Three trusted men could be released
To visit us on Boxing Day,
To share our home and join the feast.

Then they came, their hated accents
Badged them as our enemies,
Spoke of normal, human things,
Of home, and work and Christmas trees;

Talked about their country's customs,
What their families used to do –
I hadn't realised the Germans
Celebrated Christmas too.

Every Christmas after that
My Grandpa heard from Germany;
Every Christmas I recall
His lesson in humanity.

Thomas Robbins was my Grandpa,
Loved the world, despite its sin,
Looked upon the hated stranger,
Recognised the soul within.

The Drowned Boy

The drowned boy is a fish in heaven,
soaring through a rainbow sea,
free of weight and work and worry,
diving through infinity.

The drowned boy was my friend,
I lost him,
we were playing in the bay,
then a hard, unheeding current
tore apart the shining day.

The drowned boy was my brother, growing
side by side,
we loved and fought,
now I stand alone, abandoned,
in a space I never sought.

The drowned boy was my son,
I bore him,
cradled him and gave him life,
now the absence of his footsteps
cuts me like a madman's knife.

The drowned boy was my lad,
I raised him
with a father's love and pride,
now a stone is placed upon me,
by an accidental tide.

Yet he visits us in sleeping,
comforts us with arcs of bright,
effortless and endless movement,
through the oceans of the night.

Now his body is recovered,
earth enfolds the waterboy,
but we dream him free,
we see him
swim with light and swim with joy.

The Klim Monitor

I went to school in different days,
we did things in more formal ways,
we sat in silent, tidy rows,
but we were cared for, I suppose;
they gave us daily milk to drink,
to help us grow and work and think.

When Stuart started at our school,
we saw at once, he was no fool,
with laughing face and shining eyes,
and yet we learnt, to our surprise,
that though he seemed both brave and bright,
the lad could hardly read or write:
he wrote his words the wrong way round,
he could not link the shape to sound,
he could not make the words obey,
he could not write what he could say,
he gained a sort of awful fame –
the boy who could not spell his name!

We simply could not understand,
he showed us skill with eye and hand,
in sport he was an able boy,
his drawings were a source of joy,
his singing sweet to charm the birds
(if someone helped him with the words),
yet still his writing made you think
of spiders playing splash with ink.

We made it clear to him we cared,
and yet we all knew he despaired,
he thought himself both dim and dense,
because the words would not make sense.
Miss Graham tried the best she could
to help him see himself as good,
she gave him special things to do –
collecting books and mixing glue,
he wrote, 'i em a bakdraw yob
so mis as givin mi a job.'

But still, despite the friends he had
poor Stuart felt ashamed and sad,
a boy with such a clever mind,
to be so very far behind,
and then Miss Graham said she'd heard
that Stuart was to be *transferred*.

We had one week with him and then
we never saw the lad again.

Yet still today I picture him –
old Struat givin out the klim.

A Christmas Wish

If I could change the me you see,
then best of all I'd like to be
the fairy on the Christmas tree;
In tinselled net and silver lace,
with fairy wings and angel face,
I'd sit up there in pride of place;
I'd glitter for a little while,
then smile a twinkly, sparkly smile,
in special festive season style,
and everyone would aah and ooh,
and whisper, 'Is it really you?'
and I'd say, *Yes, it's really true,*
it's little
       lovely
         me.

But as it is, I'm big and strong,
my feet stick out, my hair's all wrong,
I'm less Fay Wray and more King Kong;
I've never been the sort of girl
with sticky-outy skirts that swirl,
I cannot turn a fairy twirl,
I cannot fly with fairy grace,
I haven't got a fairy face
(in fact, I wear a metal brace);
yet, though no-one would ever guess,
I know that with the proper dress
and training, I could, nonetheless
transform the lumpen lass you see
and flutter up there on that tree,
that fairest of the fair would be,
little
     lovely
        me.

My Grandmammy

My Grandmammy onetime was a skippygal like me,
learning all her letters and her
duty;
And then she flowered like the Jacaranda tree,
attracting all the suitors with her
beauty;
She left her home and travelled on a boat on the sea,
that took her to a cold, cold
country;
She was seeking for her fortune, but she met adversity,
still she never let her piccanin go
hungry;
She mother-loved my mother and my mother mothered me,
so that's my very personal
hist'ry;
And when I am a mother then her spirit may be free,
and that's a very powerful
myst'ry;
Now sometime I will be as wrinkleface as she,
I'll be sitting with my knitting and my
mem'ry,
But in the inbetweentime I'm as glad as I can be,
that my Grandmammy dear's here
with me!

Teacher's Pet

Teacher's pet is a squirt and a soppy-clogs,
and teacher's pet is a sneak,
and teacher's pet gets some kind of special job
every day of the week,
and teacher's pet gets good marks for everything,
and teacher's pet is a bore,
and teacher's pet is sickly and simpery,
and goody-girly to the core.

And me, I sit in the back row for every class,
and me, I tell rude jokes,
and me, I don't get good marks for anything,
and me, I'm one of the blokes –
so why do I feel stupid and stuttery
and what's this pain I get,
that makes me go all floozy and fluttery –
at a smile from teacher's pet?

Magic Granny

I've got a magic granny,
I keep her up a tree,
and nobody can see her there
except the birds and me.

I've got a magic granny,
I keep her on a shelf,
I have to help her up there
but she climbs down by herself.

I've got a magic granny,
I keep her in my shoe,
it isn't very comfy
but she says she likes the view.

I've got a magic granny,
I keep her in my hat,
I used to give her chocolate
but she said she got too fat.

I've got a magic granny,
I keep her by my bed,
she tells me scary stories
and she dances on my head.

I've got a magic granny,
I keep her up my nose
it isn't too hygienic,
but I'll miss her when she goes.

I've got a magic granny,
one day we'll have to part,
but even when she says it's time
she found some other tree to climb,
and when our secret shelf is bare

71

Other great reads from **Red Fox**

Further Red Fox titles that you might enjoy reading are listed on the following pages. They are available in bookshops or they can be ordered directly from us.

If you would like to order books, please send this form and the money due to:

ARROW BOOKS, BOOKSERVICE BY POST, PO BOX 29, DOUGLAS, ISLE OF MAN, BRITISH ISLES. Please enclose a cheque or postal order made out to Arrow Books Ltd for the amount due, plus 75p per book for postage and packing to a maximum of £7.50, both for orders within the UK. For customers outside the UK, please allow £1.00 per book.

NAME_____

ADDRESS_____

_____

Please print clearly.

Whilst every effort is made to keep prices low, it is sometimes necessary to increase cover prices at short notice. If you are ordering books by post, to save delay it is advisable to phone to confirm the correct price. The number to ring is THE SALES DEPARTMENT 071 (if outside London) 973 9700.

Other great reads from **Red Fox**

Have a chuckle with Red Fox Fiction!

FLOSSIE TEACAKE'S FUR COAT   Hunter Davies

Flossie just wants to be grown-up, like her big sister Bella – and when she tries on the mysterious fur coat she finds in Bella's bedroom, her wildest dreams come true . . .
ISBN 0 09 996710 3   £2.99

SNOTTY BUMSTEAD   Hunter Davies

Snotty's mum has gone away leaving him with lots of cash and the house to himself! Burgers for breakfast, football in the front room – and no homework! But can he keep the nosey grown-ups away?
ISBN 0 09 997710 9   £2.99

HENRY HOLLINS AND THE DINOSAUR
Willis Hall

Little did Henry think, when he found the fossilized egg at the seaside, that it was actually a fossilized DINOSAUR egg! He had even less idea that it would be no time at all before he would be travelling up the moorway on a dinosaur's back!
ISBN 0 09 911611 1   £2.99

THE LAST VAMPIRE   Willis Hall

The Hollins family are on holiday in Europe, and all goes well until they stay the night in a spooky castle, miles from nowhere. Even worse, they discover that they are in the castle belonging to Count Alucard.
ISBN 0 09 911541 7   £2.99

TRIV IN PURSUIT   Michael Coleman

One by one, the teachers at St Ethelred's School are vanishing, leaving cryptic notes behind. "Triv" Trevellyan smells something fishy going on and is determined to find out just what is happening!
ISBN 0 09 991660 6   £2.99

Other great reads ⟋ *from* **Red Fox**

Action-Packed Drama with Red Fox Fiction!

SIMPLE SIMON Yvonne Coppard

Simon isn't stupid – he's just not very good at practical things. So when Mum collapses, it's Cara, his younger sister who calls the ambulance and keeps a cool head. Simon plans to show what he can do too, in a crisis, but his plan goes frighteningly wrong . . .
ISBN 0 09 910531 4 £2.99

LOW TIDE William Mayne

Winner of the Guardian Children's Fiction Award.

The low tide at Jade Bay leaves fish on dry land and a wreck high on a rock. Is this the treasure ship the divers have been looking for? Three friends vow to find out – and find themselves swept away into adventure.
ISBN 0 09 918311 0 £3.50

THE INTRUDER John Rowe Townsend

It isn't often that you meet someone who claims to be you. But that's what happens to Arnold Haithwaite. The real Arnold has to confront the menacing intruder before he takes over his life completely.
ISBN 0 09 999260 4 £3.50

GUILTY Ruth Thomas

Everyone in Kate's class says that the local burglaries have been done by Desmond Locke's dad, because he's just come out of prison. Kate and Desmond think otherwise and set out to prove who really is *guilty*.
ISBN 0 09 918591 1 £2.99

The Pick of the Poets from Red Fox

THEM AND US
Jennifer Curry, illustrated by Susie Jenkin-Pearce

Pairs of poems – one by an adult and one by a child – on the same subject can mean very different ideas, as this warm, humorous, and sometimes surprising anthology shows.

ISBN 0 09 995110 X   £3.50

IT CAME THROUGH THE WALL
Tim Healey, illustrated by Tony Ross

What is the huge hairy horrible thing that comes through the wall one night? All is revealed in this deliciously spooky rhyme . . .

ISBN 0 09 922621 9   £2.99

FOR LAUGHING OUT LOUD
Edited by Jack Prelutsky, illustrated by Marjorie Priceman

"If you have got a funnybone, and I've no doubt you do,
Then this completely silly book is sure to tickle you!"
A collection of the funniest, silliest poems around – guaranteed to have you in giggles!

ISBN 0 09 923731 8   £6.99

SINGING DOWN THE BREADFRUIT
Pauline Stewart, illustrated by Duncan Smith

Tropical rain showers, hurricanes and bluebottles, coconuts and mangoes: all the smells, sounds and colours of the Caribbean are vividly captured in Pauline Stewart's first collection of poetry.

ISBN 0 09 928821 4   £3.50

WONDERCRUMP POETRY
Various prize-winning children

All the best entries from the NECA/Dahl Foundation/School Book Fairs Poetry Competition are in this wonderful new collection of poems, covering such wide-ranging topics as school, the family and growing up . . .

ISBN 0 09 930328 0   £3.50

Other great reads from **Red Fox**

Giggle and groan with a Red Fox humour book!

Nutty, naughty and quite quite mad, the Red Fox humour list has a range of the silliest titles you're likely to see on a bookshelf! Check out some of our weird and wonderful books and we promise you'll have a ribticklingly good read!

MIAOW! THE CAT JOKE BOOK – Susan Abbott

Be a cool cat and paws here for the purrfect joke! Get your claws into this collection of howlers all about our furry friends that will have you feline like a grinning Cheshire Cat!

ISBN 0 09 998460 1 £1.99

THE SMELLY SOCKS JOKE BOOK – Susan Abbott

Hold your nose . . . here comes the funniest and foulest joke book you're likely to read for a while! Packed with pungent puns and reeking with revolting riddles, this one is guaranteed to leave you gasping for air!

ISBN 0 09 956270 7 £1.99

TUTANKHAMUN IS A BIT OF A MUMMY'S BOY – Michael Coleman

Have you ever dreaded taking home your school report or a letter from the Head? You're in good company! Did you know that Shakespeare was really "hopeless at English" and that Christopher Columbus had "absolutely no sense of direction"? There's fifty other previously unpublished school reports which reveal hilarious secrets about the famous which not many people know . . .

ISBN 0 09 988180 2 £2.99

THE FISH AND CHIPS JOKE BOOK – Ian Rylett

This book comes complete with a fish-and-chips scratch and sniff panel so you can sniff while you snigger at this delicious collection of piping-hot pottiness! Your tastebuds will be tickled no end with this mouth-watering concoction of tasty gags so tuck into a copy today! It's a feast of fun!

ISBN 0 09 995040 5 £2.99

Other great reads from **Red Fox**

Discover the wacky world of Spacedog and Roy by Natalie Standiford

Spacedog isn't really a dog at all – he's an alien lifeform from the planet Queekrg, who just happens to *look* like a dog. It's a handy form of disguise – but he's not sure he'll *ever* get used to the food!

SPACEDOG AND ROY

Roy is quite surprised to find an alien spacecraft in his garden – but that's nothing to the surprise he gets when Spacedog climbs out.

ISBN 0 09 983650 5 £2.99

SPACEDOG AND THE PET SHOW

Life becomes unbearable for Spacedog when he's entered for the local pet show and a French poodle falls in love with him.

ISBN 0 09 983660 2 £2.99

SPACEDOG IN TROUBLE

When Spacedog is mistaken for a stray and locked up in the animal santuary, he knows he's in big trouble.

ISBN 0 09 983670 X £2.99

SPACEDOG THE HERO

When Roy's father goes away he makes Spacedog the family watchdog – but Spacedog is scared of the dark. What can he do?

ISBN 0 09 983680 7 £2.99

Other great reads *from* **Red Fox**

Have a bundle of fun with the wonderful Pat Hutchins

Pat Hutchins' stories are full of wild adventure and packed with outrageous humour for younger readers to enjoy.

FOLLOW THAT BUS

A school party visit to a farm ends in chaotic comedy when two robbers steal the school bus.

ISBN 0 09 993220 2 £2.99

THE HOUSE THAT SAILED AWAY

An hilarious story of a family afloat, in their house, in the Pacific Ocean. No matter what adventures arrive, Gran always has a way to deal with them.

ISBN 0 09 993200 8 £2.99

RATS!

Sam's ploys to persuade his parents to let him have a pet rat eventually meet with success, and with Nibbles in the house, life is never the same again.

ISBN 0 09 993190 7 £2.50

Join the RED FOX Reader's Club

The Red Fox Reader's Club is for readers of all ages. All you have to do is ask your local bookseller or librarian for a Red Fox Reader's Club card. As an official Red Fox Reader you only have to borrow or buy eight Red Fox books in order to qualify for your own Red Fox Reader's Clubpack – full of exciting surprises! If you have any difficulty obtaining a Red Fox Reader's Club card please write to: Random House Children's Books Marketing Department, 20 Vauxhall Bridge Road, London SW1V 2SA.